MGR PUBLISHING
4953 Dundas Street, W. Suite 105,
Toronto, Ontario, M9A 1B6, Canada

This edition produced 2004 for MGR Publishing by
LITTLE TIGER PRESS
An imprint of Magi Publications, 1 The Coda Centre,
189 Munster Road, London SW6 6AW, UK
www.littletigerpress.com

Originally published in Great Britain 2004 by
Little Tiger Press, London

Text copyright © Nicola Grant 2004
Illustrations copyright © Michael Terry 2004

Chameleon's Crazy Colors

By Nicola Grant *and* Michael Terry

Deep in the rainforest all was not well. Chameleon was having trouble with his colors.

"Darn!" he said very frustrated. "I'm sitting on yellow flowers so I should be yellow. But look at me – I'm red!"

Chameleon hopped on to a stone, and turned blue with pink spots.

Walking through the grass, he went orange! It was all terribly wrong!

Monkey and Meercat strolled by. "You look a bit off-colour today!" they said.

"I'm in a color muddle!" Chameleon wailed. "I knew I shouldn't have eaten that funny-looking bug last night! What if Lion comes prowling? If I can't change color he'll see me and eat me up!"

"Take it easy!" said Monkey. "We'll help!"

"No problem!" said Meercat.

Chameleon slipped on Monkey's old banana skin and skidded into a mango tree!

"Close your eyes and think yourself a color!" said Meercat. "I am yellow, I am yellow," chanted Chameleon. He started pacing up and down. But . . . .

"WHOOAA!"

SPLAT! A big ripe mango fell on his head!

"Ouch! I am yellow now!" said Chameleon crossly.

"Well that didn't work! I need another plan."

"That's easy!" said Monkey.

"No problem!" said Meercat.

Later, as Chameleon lay deep in thought on his favorite branch, two figures tiptoed up . . . . "Lion is coming!" they shouted. "It's LION!"

"Aaargh!" Chameleon tried to turn green – but went purple! He leapt towards some purple flowers to hide . . . .

SPLASH!

Chameleon fell into the river!

Coughing and spluttering, he scrambled aboard a floating log.

"Only joking!" shouted Monkey and Meercat. "We thought if we scared you, your colors would work properly."

That night Monkey and Meercat met in secret to make more plans. "That's a great idea!" Monkey whispered. "Let's do it!"

By dawn, the pair were ready for action.

"This disguise is really scary!" Meercat said.

"The fright will definitely make Chameleon's mixed-up colors work!"

"Stand by!" hushed Monkey.

"Chameleon's coming!"

"GRRRR!"

With a great rumbling roar Monkey leapt out.

"Help, it's LION!" Chameleon gasped. He tried to turn green – but went red!

"Only me!" laughed Monkey. "Just trying to help again!"

"Great disguise," said Chameleon. "What a shame it didn't work!"

But Monkey and Meercat wouldn't give up.

"LION!" they shouted as Chameleon munched his crunchy lunch. Chameleon almost choked on his beetle. Instead of going brown, he went blue!

"LION!" screeched Meercat as Chameleon slurped a drink. Chameleon hid among some pink flowers. But everyone saw him – he was bright orange!

"It's hopeless!" Chameleon sighed.

"Hmm. Not so easy," said Monkey.

"Quite a problem!" said Meercat.

Chameleon flopped into the shade, feeling terribly worried. Nothing worked! What would he do if Lion really came?

Just then, Meercat and Monkey ran past. They looked scared. Very scared.

"Lion!" they squealed.

"Ha, ha! You don't fool me!" Chameleon laughed. But just then he heard a very loud ROARRR!

Chameleon froze. He looked up and gulped a big gulp. "GULP!"

Lion was towering over him! "What are you?" said Lion, licking his lips.

"I-I-I'm a red spotted thingy," Chameleon stuttered. "No, I'm pink and purple. Umm, now I'm red and blue *and* purple!"

Lion looked puzzled.

Suddenly Chameleon had an idea!

"I've got Funny-Coloritis!" Chameleon told Lion. "Swallow me and you'll get an upset tummy!"

"Funny-Coloritis?" growled Lion, backing away fast.

"Are you sure?"

"Oh, yes!" Chameleon said. "Eat me and you'll end up looking crazy colored like me, too!"

"Yikes!" gasped Lion, shaking with fear. "I'm out of here!" And he disappeared in a cloud of dust.

"Three cheers for clever Chameleon!" laughed Monkey. "He's gotten rid of that Lion for good!"